W9-AGI-635

ILLUMINATION PRESENTS

MINIONS
THE RISE OF GRU

THE MOVIE NOVEL

Cover design by Ching N. Chan

Little, Brown and Company
Hachette Book Group
1290 Avenue of the Americas, New York, NY 10104
Visit us at LBYR.com

First Edition: May 2022

Little, Brown and Company is a division of Hachette Book Group, Inc.
The Little, Brown name and logo are trademarks of Hachette Book Group, Inc.

Library of Congress Control Number: 2020933240

ISBNs: 978-0-316-42584-1 (paper over board), 978-0-316-42580-3 (pbk.), 978-0-316-42583-4 (ebook)

Printed in the United States of America

LSC-C

Paper over board: 10 9 8 7 6 5 4 3 2 1
Paperback: 10 9 8 7 6 5 4 3 2 1

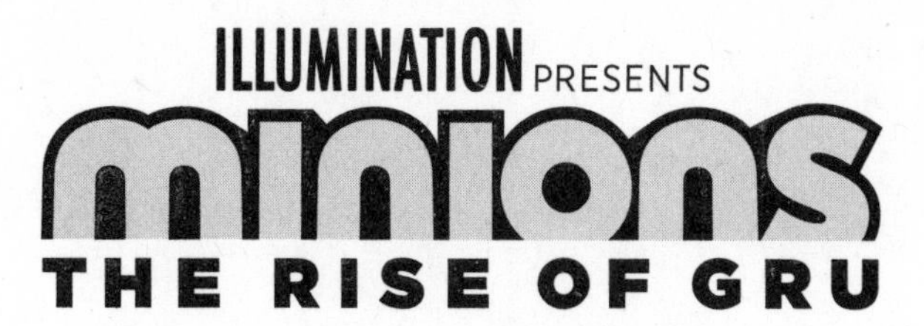

THE MOVIE NOVEL

Adapted by Sadie Chesterfield
Screenplay by Matt Fogel

Little, Brown and Company
New York • Boston

MINIONS
MINIONS

PROLOGUE

The Anti-Villain League chased the motorcycle through busy city streets. One of the agents yelled at the villain. "AVL!" he shouted, announcing himself. "Freeze!"

"Come back here!" the second agent yelled.

Belle Bottom, a tall, elegant villain in a purple jumpsuit, swerved right on her motorcycle, then left, evading them. She pressed the gas and the motorcycle zoomed forward, moving twice as fast. Soon the agents disappeared behind her.

"Woooo!" Belle Bottom laughed. "You like that?"

She turned down an alley and sped into a secret entrance of a store called Criminal Records. The motorcycle screeched to a halt, and she climbed off. Then she took the elevator to the subterranean lair.

When the doors slid back, Belle Bottom held a map in the air. The Vicious 6, one of the fiercest teams of supervillains, sat at a conference table. There was Svengeance, a hulking blond with pec muscles that could crush skulls. Nun-Chuck, who was always dressed as a nun, concealed all sorts of weapons under her long black habit. Jean-Clawed wore a striped shirt and had one regular hand and one huge red pincer. And Stronghold had a massive silver glove on each hand, which he used to pummel anyone who crossed him. Wild Knuckles was the oldest and the leader of the group.

"Hooo baby!" Belle Bottom yelled. "The Anti-Villain League can't catch this! Guess who stole the map?!"

She passed said map to Svengeance, who threw it to Jean-Clawed, who unrolled the map on the table. Wild Knuckles stared down at it, running his wrinkled hands over the paper. He'd never seen anything more beautiful in his entire life.

"Haha," he said. "Good work. The map to the legendary Zodiac Stone. We will become the most powerful villains in the world! Okay, let's get a move on! We leave for China tonight!"

His whole team cheered.

This next mission was going to be epic....

MINIONS
MINIONS

CHAPTER 1

The jungle was a dense tangle of trees and vines. Wild Knuckles soared through it with his winged jetpack contraption, weaving back and forth. He might be older than the rest of the Vicious 6, but he could still pursue evil with the best of them.

He landed in front of a massive waterfall flanked by two dragon statues. There was a rock with a small replica of the statues just a few feet ahead of him. He stared down at the map, then adjusted the replicas to match their positions to a picture hidden in the illustration. In an instant, the huge dragon statues started rumbling and breathing fire, causing the waterfall to evaporate. Where there once was water was now a doorway.

"I'm in," Wild Knuckles whispered into his headset, hoping his team could still hear him from all the way down here.

He'd done horrific, villainous things in his life. Sneaky, underhanded thievery was simple. Easy. But finding the Zodiac Stone here, in the middle of the jungle, would be a new triumph. He took a deep breath and headed inside.

Wild Knuckles went through the doorway and descended a long flight of stairs. He was trying to be careful, but he took a false step. Then the whole staircase turned into a slide. He zoomed all the way down, deep into the heart of the fortress. He just narrowly missed several razor-sharp spikes at the bottom. When Wild Knuckles finally reached the bottom of the slide, he looked up and saw the Zodiac Stone in the next room over. It was bigger than his fist—a gold thing with tiny emeralds encrusted around the edges. It sat on top of a pedestal, bathed in the light from a single window above.

"Hello, beautiful," Wild Knuckles said.

He went toward the Stone, but just as he reached to grab it, the door behind him slammed shut. Light illuminated warrior statues that encircled the room's walls. The statues started to shake, coming to life. They advanced on Wild Knuckles, as if to attack.

Wild Knuckles sprang into action, fighting them off one by one. When the last statue was vanquished, he turned and grabbed the Stone, holding it high in the air.

"Yes! The Zodiac Stone!" he yelled.

The walls around him lit up, revealing all the animals of the zodiac painted on them. The animals glowed with a strange light, then rushed off the walls and into the center of the jewels. It was as though all the power of this fortress was now locked inside the Stone.

"Soon, the power of these unstoppable beasts will be ours!" he cried.

The ceiling parted, and sunlight streamed in from above. The floor of the room rose up to the sky. Wild Knuckles put the Stone around his neck and kissed it. He'd done it. He'd really done it. He'd found the Stone all by himself.

When the floor leveled out, Wild Knuckles turned, about to run off into the jungle, when he realized he was surrounded by hundreds of golden guardians. Where had they come from? Did he really have to fight them?

Wild Knuckles wasn't given time to consider his options before the guardians took action, dog piling on top of him. Wild Knuckles struggled and managed to bust free of them. He couldn't fight them off for too long, though. Eventually they backed him up against two large bamboo poles.

Wild Knuckles scrambled up the poles, but the guardians began cutting them down. Before he could fall, Wild Knuckles took off running to the large dragon head at the top of the fortress, using the bamboo as stilts. He ditched his stilts once he reached the fortress and started climbing its exterior.

"Hurry up, I got a bunch of deadly tchotchkes on my tail!" he shouted into his headset. His team was supposed to be waiting to help him escape.

"Roger that on the copy, boss!" the voice of Belle Bottom said.

Okay . . ., he thought, relieved. *They're coming for you. But when?*

The guardians climbed onto one another's shoulders, trying to reach Wild Knuckles at the top of the fortress. He kept climbing, and eventually a rope dropped down from the sky. The Super Ship had arrived—the Vicious 6 were here. They'd come to save him!

"Hurry up! Come on!" Belle Bottom yelled down.

He grasped the rope and shot up into the air, toward the flying aircraft.

"Haha!" he yelled. "I got it! I got the Stone!"

When he was just a few feet away from the bottom of the ship, a face peered over the edge at him. Wild Knuckles was relieved to see Belle Bottom, his second in command. She reached out her arm. He reached up as well, trying to help her hoist him into the aircraft. But instead of helping him, she grabbed the Stone out of his gnarled hand.

"Party's over, old man," she said.

"Time to say goodbye!" Nun-Chuck crowed from behind Belle Bottom.

"Hold on—I started this group," Wild Knuckles shot back. "We're a team! Where's your loyalty?"

"Oh please," Belle Bottom said. "We're villains. There's no such thing."

Jean-Clawed reached down and snipped the rope with his giant crab pincer. "It's time for the next generation!"

Wild Knuckles went flying into a ravine below. Belle Bottom held up the Stone and laughed an excited, villainous laugh.

MINIONS
MINIONS

CHAPTER 2

In an ordinary elementary school on an ordinary street, an exceptionally boring teacher stood in front of a class of sixth graders. She wrote *Career Day* on the chalkboard in big block letters. Then she stared out at her students.

"So, what do you want to be when you grow up?" she asked in a monotone voice. A hand shot up in the back of the room. "Samantha?"

"I want to be a doctor," the girl replied.

She was always sucking up, telling the teacher exactly what she wanted to hear. Samantha had an answer for everything.

"Oh, me! Me!" another student cried. "I wanna be a fireman who is also the president and also drives race cars. Yeah!"

"Exciting," the teacher said, but she sounded as if she were falling asleep. "And what about you, Gru?"

The whole class turned around and studied the pale, chubby boy at the back of the class. He wasn't paying attention and was instead doodling in his notebook. He had a long, beak-like nose and always wore the same gray-and-black-striped scarf. And he had hair—a whole head of it—the thick black mop combed perfectly in place.

"Gru?" the teacher repeated.

"Me?" he replied, snapping to attention. He'd drawn himself as a member of the Vicious 6, a group of villains who were his idols. He'd sent an application to join the team ages ago, but he still hadn't heard back. He had to imagine it was just a formality. When they had an opening, they would definitely call him in for an interview.

"I want to be . . . a supervillain," Gru finally said.

He leaned back in his chair and smirked. He was going to be the baddest of the bad. The most vicious of the vicious. He couldn't wait until people saw him flying in the Vicious 6's Super Ship or scaling the Empire State Building, about to steal the needle from the top.

The class was quiet. Everyone stared at him. Then, all at once, they started laughing. A girl with blond pigtails laughed so hard she almost fell out of her chair. Gru looked around, wondering what was so funny. Would they all laugh when he robbed the National Treasury? When he took over the world?

The bell rang, and he stormed out, trying to forget all of them.

Every day after school, the Minions picked Gru up and took him on fun outings. They always tried to hug and kiss Gru, which he *hated*. The Minions usually wore their grooviest seventies outfits. They loved bell-bottoms and big sunglasses, and sometimes they styled themselves with sideburns or teased hair. That particular day, the Minions and Gru all went to the movies together to watch *Jaws*. Gru threw a Fart Grenade into the theater so they could get seats for a sold-out show. After the movie, the Minions took Gru to the arcade. They loved playing Whac-A-Mole, popping out of the machine so Gru could bop them on the head. They also loved helping Gru cheat at the arcade games, ensuring a win every time. After that, they got ice cream.

When Gru and the Minions got home, the first thing Gru did was go to the mailbox, just as he did every day. He riffled through bills addressed to his mom, some meditation magazines, and some junk mail, finally stopping on a manila envelope that read MR. GRU. He ripped the envelope open. Inside was an 8-track tape from the Vicious 6!

"Holy guacamole!" Gru yelled, turning to the Minions. "Where can we listen? Where can we listen?"

He looked around, frantic. He spotted his mom's car across the driveway. He ran to the car and jumped inside, shoving the plastic cartridge into the player. The Minions all crammed in next to him. They watched as a hologram of Belle Bottom materialized.

"Hello, Mr. Gru," Belle Bottom said. "We've received your application to the world's best supervillain team, the Vicious 6."

Bob, one of the Minions, was confused by the hologram and kept trying to grab it. Stuart, another Minion, had to physically restrain him to get him to stop. Belle Bottom continued.

"A recent opening has become available and..."

"And?!" Gru yelled, unable to wait for her to finish the sentence.

"Your interview is tomorrow at noon," she said.

"Woo-hooo!" Gru yelled. "Dy-no-mite!"

"Dy-no-mite!" the Minions repeated.

"Please go to 417 Main Street. The password is 'You're no good,' " Belle Bottom explained.

"You're no good," Gru read the words as they appeared in the hologram. He loved how they sounded. "Hmmm."

"Now get on up on the downstroke, 'cause this invitation is gonna explode, baby!" Belle Bottom said.

"Explode?" Gru asked, glancing at the Minions. "No, no, no..."

He reached for the door, but before he could get out, the tape exploded in a cloud of smoke. The Minions darted out of the car, coughing and hacking, their little lungs hurting. Bob choo-chooed like a train. Every time he opened his mouth, a puff of gray smoke flew out.

After dusting themselves off, the Minions followed Gru to his bedroom. The walls were covered in Vicious 6 posters, and tiny figurines of his heroes lined his desk. He had Vicious 6 hats and Vicious 6 underwear. Whenever he wore them, he felt powerful.

"Come on, let's go tell the troops the good news," Gru said, leading the Minions into his closet. He grabbed an empty hanger and yanked hard, releasing a trapdoor. Gru and the Minions flew down a long slide and into the bunker below.

The Minions were still finishing Gru's evil lair. They hummed and whistled while they worked, hammering away and pouring concrete. Gru looked around at their progress.

"This is fantastic! Oh, construction looks great, guys!" he said. "My first evil lair. Goose bumps!"

A Minion walked past with dynamite. Just seconds later, something exploded. Gru watched as two Minions rushed past him with a stretcher. He laughed nervously.

"Well, you gotta break a few eggs to make an omelet, am I right?" he said.

He walked over to Ryan, a Minion jackhammering away at the earth, breaking up giant chunks of rock.

"Great job, Ryan!" he yelled at the top of his lungs.

"What?" Ryan yelled back.

"I said, great job!" Gru screamed even louder. But when Ryan didn't hear, Gru just said, "Never mind."

"Joe, how's the family?" Gru called to a Minion lighting a blowtorch. Before Joe could respond, the blowtorch blasted the little guy in the face, burning off his eyebrows. Gru just tip-toed away. It was more than a little awkward.

"Okay, everybody, get over here," Gru said to the Minions. "Now listen up. Buckle your overalls. Hold on to your goggles. . . . The Vicious 6 want to meet me! Tomorrow!"

A chant started somewhere in the back of the crowd and grew louder. "Mini Boss! Mini Boss!" the Minions cheered.

"All right, all right!" Gru finally said. "I'm not a mini! Please stop calling me that. And also, they haven't accepted me yet."

A short, round Minion with a mouthful of

braces came up to Gru. His name was Otto, and he immediately started babbling. He launched into an extremely long, and kind of annoying, pep talk in gibberish. Gru just stood there and politely listened.

"Blah blah blah...," Kevin said, making fun of Otto.

"Yes... *mmmhmmm*...," Gru said, hoping Otto would stop on his own.

But the Minion kept going, rambling on with words Gru only half understood. He said something about Gru being the evilest and the Vicious 6 being lucky to have him.

"*Oooookay*," Gru said, interrupting. "You know what would be fun? Let's play the quiet game!"

Otto nodded and closed his mouth. But every few seconds he'd open it again, as if he were about to say something else. It was almost impossible for him to stop talking completely.

"Anyway," Gru went on. "Thanks for the

hard work today, everyone. I gotta go get some rest—tomorrow is the biggest day of my life!"

Gru hopped onto a ladder, which raised him back up to his room. The whole time Gru got ready for bed, he kept imagining himself in the Vicious 6. Laughing and chatting with them in their Super Ship. Going on long, faraway missions to the Bermuda Triangle or to steal the Great Wall of China.

He had a whole speech planned out. He'd been rehearsing it for months, ever since he first sent in his application. He wanted to tell them how long he'd admired their work. He was going to tell them about his evil lair and how he'd spent his whole short life preparing to be the baddest of the bad.

Gru climbed into his bed and turned out the light. He knew he needed a good night's sleep so he would be ready for tomorrow's interview. But he couldn't resist shining his flashlight onto a poster of the Vicious 6 so he could see them one last time.

"Oh, these guys are the best," he said. "Can't believe it."

He heard a sound in his closet. When he moved the flashlight, he lit up Bob, who'd climbed up from the lair. Bob was in his pajamas, and his eyes were wide, as if he were frightened.

"Uh, Mini Boss?" Bob asked. "No la ti pa todo . . . para tu?"

He wanted to cuddle. Normally, Gru would tell him to hop on in bed, and they'd sleep next to each other, but he had the biggest interview of his life tomorrow morning. He didn't want to smell Bob's farts all night.

"Yeah, I get it," Gru said. "But I need a good night's sleep, so get out."

"Oh," Bob said sullenly. "Me ya la naci korang. Que sa panise."

"Okay, fine, fine." Gru caved. "Because you had a nightmare. But just tonight."

The Minion smiled as he climbed into bed next to Gru. He tucked himself beneath the covers and fell fast asleep. But it wasn't long before another Minion appeared from the closet. Kevin stood there, hoping to get into bed as well.

"Ah scusa?" he said. "Eh mi? Para de vidal por ma de vio."

"Oh really? You too?" Gru said, skeptical. He was not buying this whole nightmare story. "Get in."

Kevin snuggled right next to him, on his other side. Gru tried to get comfortable, but the bed was too full. Every time he tried to turn over, there was nowhere to go.

"Boodnight," Bob said happily.

"Boodnight," Kevin added, snuggling even closer.

"Yes, yes, yes," Gru said. "Good night."

Then Stuart emerged from the closet and did a running leap onto the bed.

"Boodnight!" he yelled.

"I just want to get some sleep . . . ," Gru tried.

How was he supposed to be ready for his big interview if the Minions wouldn't give him a second alone? Gru closed his eyes, but he could feel the Minions practically on top of him. Kevin's butt was on his arm, which was now numb. Stuart kept kicking him as he tried to get comfortable. Bob was the worst, though. He hadn't even been in bed ten minutes and the gas had already started.

Gru groaned, then closed his eyes. *Just think of the Vicious 6*, he told himself. After a few minutes, he started to dream of pulling off a diamond heist with them. A smile spread over his face, and he slowly drifted off to sleep.

CHAPTER 3

The next morning, Gru sprang out of bed. He jumped into the shower and washed his hair, even though he hated washing his hair. He scrubbed under his armpits and behind his ears. He dried himself off and combed his hair so it sat perfectly in place. Then he put on his Vicious 6 underwear. They made him feel as if he were already part of the team.

"*I see a bad Gru arising*," he sang as he pulled

on the rest of his clothes. *"I see a villain on his way. I'm gonna interview with my heroes. They're gonna love me 'cause I'm the best. Don't mess up tonight! You're going to join the Vicious 6!"*

Gru strolled out of his house, feeling better than he had in weeks. His dream was finally coming true. He was going to be a villain—one of the evilest villains in the world. No one at school would laugh at him then.

"*Here is the bad Gru on the rise . . .*," he sang softly.

He didn't get more than two steps before he ran smack into Bob, Kevin, and Stuart. They were standing on the front porch, waiting for him.

"Puncha-meena-toba," Kevin said. "Pinta-view."

"Oh . . ." Gru nodded. "You want to come."

The Minions nodded excitedly. Bob jumped up and down. Gru knew the Minions could be relentless when they wanted something. When the Minions responded to Gru's "Help Wanted" ad, they wouldn't take no for an answer. They even stood vigil in the rain to convince Gru to hire them! Of course, it turned out that the "rain" was just water from a hose, but it worked on Gru all the same.

"Right... okay, guys...," Gru started. "Here's the thing.... The Vicious 6, they're the big leagues. And you guys... are great... and so... the job you did on the lair, A-plus."

The Minions stared at him, wondering where this was going.

"It's just...," Gru continued. "What I was thinking is, there are a lot of other villains in the world. You know?"

"No. Porque?" Bob said. No, he didn't know.

Gru let out a deep breath. This was going to be harder than he thought it would be. The

Minions weren't getting it. They really were not getting it.

"Never mind. Look," Gru went on. "I think I just need to fly solo on this."

The Minions were still staring at him as if he'd just smacked them across the face. Gru kept talking and tried to keep it positive. This wasn't goodbye forever. It was just goodbye for . . . well, maybe it was ever. But he had the Vicious 6 now. Who cared about the Minions?! Soon he'd be laughing it up with Belle Bottom or doing bench presses with Stronghold.

"See you later, alligators!" Gru called over his shoulder. Then he strode down the front stairs and climbed onto his bike. He sped off, ignoring the Minions staring after him. Gru could think only of the Vicious 6 and his big interview. He kept going over what he would say.

In just two hours, he'd be one of the most powerful villains in the world!

CHAPTER 4

Wild Knuckles stared at his television set. He'd been watching the Villain Network Channel, the only thing that made him forget how terrible the past few days had been. His so-called team had left him in the jungle to die. They'd betrayed him, stolen the Zodiac Stone, which *he'd* found, and kicked him out of his own crew.

It had taken him forever to get out of that jungle. He had the bug bites to prove it. Now that he was back home, he couldn't stop thinking about how he'd get revenge on his "friends." Yeah, he was old and had a bad back and knees, but he wasn't going to let that stop him from retrieving his treasure.

"Breaking news from one of the grooviest villain teams in the world... the Vicious 6!" an anchor said, appearing on-screen.

Wild Knuckles's stomach dropped. Belle Bottom stood in front of a backdrop with the Vicious 6 logo.

"Villains of the world! In three days, when the clock strikes midnight and the Chinese New Year begins, this bad boy's power is going to be unleashed!" Belle Bottom held up the Zodiac Stone—the very stone *he* had stolen. "With the power of the zodiac, we're going to take out the Anti-Villain League—and the Vicious 6 will be the most powerful villains on the planet. Can you dig it?!"

Wild Knuckles couldn't take it anymore. He kicked the TV and knocked it over.

"Do I dig it?" he repeated. "Do I *dig* it? I *don't* dig it. There's nothing to dig! They thought they could leave me for dead, huh?"

He turned to the three henchmen standing in the corner of his living room. They weren't as good as the Vicious 6, but hey—beggars can't be choosers.

"Kick me to the curb like a piece of old meat?" Wild Knuckles said, annoyed. "Oh, they got no idea what's coming! Ha!"

"Um...Mr. Knuckles?" one of the henchmen asked.

But Wild Knuckles was so furious he barely heard him.

"Oh, I'm going to make them suffer for what they did to me," he raged on.

"Hey...Mr. Knuckles?" the henchman repeated.

"WHAT?!" Wild Knuckles roared.

"We, uh, just wanted to make sure we'd be getting paid this week," another said.

"What a mouth on you," Wild Knuckles snapped. "I'm paying you with knowledge!"

"You are?" the first henchman asked.

Wild Knuckles smacked him hard across the face.

"Lesson one: Always be prepared!" He laughed.

The first henchman ran forward, and they began to spar. Every time the henchman tried to throw a punch, Wild Knuckles blocked it. The old man kept getting into the henchman's space, landing blows to his ribs and legs.

"Lesson two," Wild Knuckles yelled as he blocked another punch. "The Belgian Five-Armed Nose Pick."

His hands were everywhere. For a brief moment, it looked as if Wild Knuckles had five arms. He jammed his fingers into the henchman's nose, eyes, and ears.

"And lesson three: the Lithuanian Hair Cut!" Wild Knuckles laughed.

Wild Knuckles reached into the henchman's collar and ripped off a patch of his chest hair. The henchman wailed in pain. Wild Knuckles looked down at the pile of black curls in the palm of his hand and blew it all right into the henchman's face. The man stumbled backward, trying to brush it out of his mouth.

"That's worth all the money in the world." Wild Knuckles laughed.

But the three henchmen looked less than convinced. The one guy was still rubbing at his chest, where there was now a giant pink patch.

"Hey, guys, fuggadaboutit." Wild Knuckles laughed. "You're gonna get paid. But first, we gotta get the Stone back."

MINI×NS
MINI×NS

CHAPTER 5

Gru repeated the address in his head the entire ride there. He wasn't able to write it down, and it would've been too risky anyway, so he memorized it. When he finally pulled up in front of 417 Main Street, he was surprised to see a record store. CRIMINAL RECORDS read the sign above the door.

He strode inside, searching for anyone who looked as if they might be in charge. Dozens of people milled about, thumbing through vinyl records and 8-tracks. There was no clear entrance to the Vicious 6's lair, though he knew it would be carefully hidden. Who was he supposed to say the password to? How was he supposed to know how to use it?

He spotted a huge, muscular guy looking through some records. Gru walked over to him and tried to seem nonchalant.

"Hello there," he said, all friendly. "Excuse me, sir?"

The man glared at him, his cheeks bright red. He looked as if he wanted to break Gru in half.

Gru continued, "I just was wondering if... *you're no good*?"

That really seemed to anger the man. He was twice the size of Gru, and he leaned down, getting right in his face. He growled like a rabid dog.

"Oh," Gru said sweetly. "You're good. My mistake."

Gru tiptoed away, grateful he hadn't gotten pummeled. But when he turned around, trying to figure out where to go next, he was completely confused. Where was the entrance to the Vicious 6's hideout? Why would they tell him to go here if it wasn't clear?

WHAM!

He felt something cool and sticky on his cheek. He looked down and noticed a thick, green, sticky hand.

"Gah!" he yelled, trying to shake it off.

A man with an oval face and a sharp, pointy nose stood behind him.

"Oh, sorry!" he said. "I didn't mean to scare you. I was just trying out this new invention of mine. I call it 'Sticky Hand,' or 'Smart Goo.' I haven't quite landed on the name yet."

The man flicked his wrist, and the Sticky Hand flew back, away from Gru.

"Come here," he whispered, a sneaky smile curling on his lips. "I heard you were looking for something... special."

"Ah yes!" Gru said, relieved. "I was hoping... *you're no good.*"

The man slipped behind the counter and retrieved something, then passed it to Gru. It was a vinyl record.

"I think you'll enjoy listening in booth three," the man said. "Right this way...."

Gru stared at the record in his hands. He was so excited about his interview, the Vicious 6, and this weird but evil-seeming man who was helping him, that he didn't notice the four tiny faces pressed against the record store's front window. Kevin, Stuart, Bob, and Otto had followed him there.

The man led Gru to a booth with an OUT OF

ORDER sign. The booth had folding glass doors and contained a record player.

"This is it," the man said, waving Gru inside. "Mum's the word. Keep it down. Good luck! Let 'em have it, son."

"Thanks, Mr."—Gru peered down at the man's name tag—"Nefario."

"That's *Doctor* Nefario," the man corrected him. He passed Gru the sticky hand thing. "Here, take this. And if you ever get famous, remember who gave you your first gadget."

"Okay," Gru said, but he was so focused on the record that he just wanted this Dr. Nefario to go away. He slipped the vinyl disc onto the record player and set the needle on top of it. The song "You're No Good" by Linda Ronstadt came on. He waited a minute, but nothing happened.

Dr. Nefario tapped on the glass.

"Try backwards," he said, pointing to the record.

Gru pressed his finger down on the record and started rotating it in the opposite direction. The music stopped. Instead, there was a secret message. A man's voice said, "Welcome to the Vicious 6. . . ."

The listening booth suddenly transformed into an elevator, and Gru was sent flying downward into the depths of the building. He landed with a *thud*. The doors opened to a waiting room packed with villains. Everyone sat in threatening, stone-faced silence. One especially menacing villain was sharpening a giant cleaver.

"Hello? Everybody here for an interview?" Gru asked. No one responded. "Me too."

He walked over to an empty chair and plopped down, but his stomach was doing somersaults. Now that he was finally here, he'd never been so nervous in his life. What order were they being called in? Was what he was wearing okay? He had to remember to stand up straight, because when he hunched, he looked smaller than he actually was. They probably didn't want a small villain.

"So what do you guys got going on later?" he asked, glancing around at his fellow interviewees. "Are you up to no good? You gonna get into some mischief?"

A minute passed, and still no one said anything to him. The silence was driving Gru insane. All he could think about was how nervous he was and what he was going to say. How was he going to impress them?

He turned to the massive villain next to him. "What do you drive? I got a Jet Bike."

An intercom buzzed, and a familiar voice echoed through the room.

"Send the first one in," Belle Bottom said.

The secretary looked at Gru. "They're ready to see you, Mr. Gru."

"Oh good. Great," Gru mumbled, but he felt terrible.

He stood and opened the door. The Vicious 6 sat at the end of a long walkway. As soon as Gru saw them, his heart started pounding in his chest. His throat was dry. He could barely breathe.

He took one step, then another, his mind completely blank. He was so focused on the team that he nearly walked right off the walkway. When Gru was finally right in front of them, he remembered the speech he'd rehearsed a hundred times in his bedroom. He had to say it. His time was now.

Gru straightened his scarf and sweater.

"Distinguished villains!" he said. "My name is Gru. I feel like I'm talking too loud, even though our proximity doesn't require this kind of volume."

The Vicious 6 all stared at him. They didn't smile. They didn't even blink.

"If you'd told me when I was ten that I would have the chance to fill the shoes of my favorite villain ever, Wild Knuckles," he went on, "I would have said you got rocks in your head. But now that I'm eleven and three quarters, it makes a lot more sense."

Belle Bottom turned toward the door, annoyed. "All right, who let the kid in?"

"I thought he was a tiny man!" Jean-Clawed laughed. He smacked his claw on the table.

Belle Bottom narrowed her eyes at Gru. "What's wrong with you? You seriously think a puny little child can be a villain?"

"Um. Yes," Gru said. "I—I am pretty despicable. You don't want to cross me."

"Evil is for adults," Belle Bottom continued. She hit a button, and suddenly a panel in the wall behind her slid back, displaying the Zodiac Stone. "Adults who steal powerful, ancient stones and wreak havoc, and not for tubby little punks who should be at school! Learning. Taking a recess. Sucking his thumb."

The Vicious 6 laughed. It started out small, but then they were really cracking up. The laughter echoed in Gru's ears. He wished he could just fall into the floor and disappear. He'd never wanted to be somewhere else so badly.

"Come back when you've done something to impress me," Belle Bottom said when she'd finally stopped laughing. Then she stared out the door, looking at something behind him. "Who's next?"

CHAPTER 6

Gru tried not to cry. He turned and started walking out, and the next villain strolled in past him. He was a round man in a skintight pink jumpsuit.

"I am Wing Man!" the guy yelled. "The next member of the Vicious 6! Behold the power of flight!"

He spread his arms out wide, but nothing happened. The Vicious 6 stared at him, but then, in an instant, he blasted off toward the ceiling. He was out of control, though. He zigzagged across the room in weird, uneven bursts.

Belle Bottom pulled out a lasso and tried to rope him in, but it was no use. The man's rockets were too strong. The other members of the Vicious 6 helped her, and they all tugged on the rope together. Gru stood near the desk, his eyes locked on the Zodiac Stone. They were all so distracted by Wing Man that they'd left their most valuable possession unprotected.

Gru pulled out the Sticky Hand Dr. Nefario had given him. He tried to use it, but it smacked him in the face, putting him flat on his back on the floor. Gru stood up and tried again, flinging the hand across the room. This time he managed to grab the Stone. Then he darted for the exit.

The Vicious 6 were still wrestling Wing Man to the ground. They managed to get him onto their desk, but then Belle Bottom caught a glimpse of the empty display. She turned to the exit and spotted Gru, running with something tucked under his arm.

"He took the Stone!" Belle Bottom yelled.

"I'll get him!" Stronghold roared. He pummeled his giant boxing gloves against the walkway, making it crumble. But Gru was just quick enough. He made it to the end before the ground could collapse under him, and then he slipped out the door.

"Lock down the building," Belle Bottom commanded.

Gru had made it up the elevator and out of the listening booth when the alarm sounded. The music playing in the record store stopped. All the customers who'd been milling about turned and stared at Gru.

"I didn't—I—" he muttered. Then he stuck the Stone under his jacket. "Nothing to see here."

He tried to be casual. He walked out of the store, checking out a few albums on the way before bumping into a man. It was Dr. Nefario, and he was staring at Gru. For a second, Gru was convinced that was the end, that Nefario would bust him. Then the man smiled a sneaky, underhanded smile.

"Just keep walking…," he whispered.

Gru nodded and strode out of Criminal Records. He dashed across the street to his bike. He'd almost reached it when he heard a familiar giggling. He turned back and saw Kevin, Stuart, Bob, and Otto standing at the curb.

"Bello!" Kevin called out.

"Mini Boss!" Otto said. He ran to Gru, his arms outstretched for a hug.

"What are you doing here?" Gru yelled.

Otto launched into one of his long, boring explanations, rambling on and on.

"Okay, just get on!" he said, knowing it would go for two hours if he didn't interrupt. He waved the Minions onto the back of his Jet Bike. It seemed like forever before he could finally take off.

The Vicious 6 sprang out of Criminal Records and chased after them. Svengeance pulled ahead, racing out on his roller skates, and soon he was right behind Gru. Gru turned down an alley, trying to lose him. Kevin knocked over some trash cans to try to slow Svengeance down, but nothing worked. He was so huge he just leaped over them as if they were soda cans.

Gru spotted a door in the alley and banged his fist on it as they rode past. "Knock, knock! Delivery!" he yelled.

Someone inside opened the door, and—*BAM!*—Svengeance slammed right into it. There was no time to celebrate, though—Gru and the Minions were headed right toward a narrow set of stairs that led to a street below. The bike sailed off the top step, and they all went tumbling down, the bike wildly cart-wheeling with them. The ride was so bumpy that Otto and the Stone flew off the back of the bike and hit the pavement.

They couldn't stop. The rest of the Vicious 6 had already appeared behind Gru, racing up a side street. Gru turned back to Otto.

"Otto, take the Stone back to the lair!" he yelled. "I'll distract them! Go, go, go!"

Following orders, Otto took the Stone and ran in the other direction. Gru and the rest of the Minions zoomed down the street on his bike, weaving between cars and people. He pressed a button on his dashboard, trying to switch the jet engines into high gear, but it didn't work. Just then, Bob tapped Gru's shoulder. He pointed to Stronghold, who was on the street up ahead. Nun-Chuck, Belle Bottom, and Jean-Clawed were closing in behind them. They were trapped.

Stronghold picked up a van and tossed it at Gru as if it were a paper cup. Nun-Chuck threw her namesake nunchucks right at Gru's head. Somehow Gru dodged both things, and the nunchucks hit Stronghold. The van collided with Nun-Chuck, knocking her out. Gru zoomed forward, hoping it would give him the opening he needed.

"I'll handle this!" Belle Bottom yelled from somewhere behind them.

She deployed her ball-and-chain device, which flew out into the sky and looped around the back of Gru's bike. She held on tight and glided along behind the bike, with Jean-Clawed on the chain right behind her. It wouldn't be long before she slowed Gru to a stop, and the Stone would be hers again.

"Hope you enjoy the rest of your short life," she said, laughing.

Gru pressed the button again and again, trying to make the jet engines work. Why hadn't he made the Minions repair it when he first realized it was broken?

"Please work," he said. "Come on, come on, come on, come on."

He jammed the button down with his fist, and finally the engines sprang to life. In one big blast, he zoomed forward, going five times the speed he had been going before. Jean-Clawed dragged his giant crab claw along the pavement, trying desperately to slow them down. But that only made the chain connecting them to the bike tighten and then snap in two. Belle Bottom glided to a smooth stop while Jean-Clawed tumbled backward into some nearby cars.

“We’re coming for you, tiny man!” Jean-Clawed yelled.

Gru could barely hear him over the rush of his jet engines. The bike was going its fastest, and the Minions clung tight to Gru as they weaved in and out of traffic, toward home. He was so happy he didn’t even notice the orange van that turned and started following him. It stayed right behind him, turning left when he went left and straight when he went straight, until it stopped where he stopped—just a few yards from his house.

MINIONS
MINIONS

CHAPTER 7

"They all said a kid couldn't be a real villain," Gru said, staring out at the adoring crowd of Minions. "Well, this kid just stole something from the worst villains in the world!"

The Minions cheered and jumped up and down. Two Minions were DJing. They played "We Are the Champions" by Queen, and all the Minions swayed back and forth with the music.

"When I bring it back to them," Gru went on, "they are going to say: *We have made a terrible mistake. Please join us. Please, Gru.* And I will say: *Yes, I will be the newest member of the Vicious 6*! Now all I need is Otto!" He glanced around the lair, looking for the bug-eyed Minion. "Where's Otto?"

"Otto le komay," Kevin said.

"No, not 'Otto le komay,'" Gru said, annoyed. "He needs to komay now."

"Bazoookaaaaa!" a tiny voice yelled. Otto slid down into the lair.

"There you are!" Gru said, relieved. "You got it?"

"Si, si, si." Otto reached into his pocket and pulled out . . . a rock. It had googly eyes glued on one side. It was some kid's toy, not the beautiful stone Gru had stolen from the most powerful villains in the world.

"Is this . . ." Gru furrowed his brows. "Are

you pulling on my legs right now? Otto, where's the Stone?"

"Le skone?" Otto asked. "Ah, si, skone. Ooo. Big a-storia."

Otto started rambling, going on and on about how he was walking down the street when he tripped and fell into a mud puddle. The Stone got stuck in the mud, but when he tried to pull it out, it flew out of his hands and down a Slip 'N Slide. He chased it and fumbled with the Stone as they slid down the Slip 'N Slide together. Then the Stone landed on a duck. A real live duck. Otto wrestled with the duck, and the duck attacked him. Then the duck flew away, and the Stone fell on Otto's head. After this all happened, he realized he was in the middle of a child's birthday party.

As he looked around, taking in the scene, he saw the birthday boy through the window. He was inside, unwrapping a present. He pulled a rock with googly eyes out of a box. Its eyes googled at Otto. Otto googled his eyes back. Then he ran inside the house and traded the Stone for his new pet. That rock was the coolest thing he'd ever seen!

Otto held it up in front of Gru and shook it back and forth, getting the eyes to google.

"Tu pissimo, no?" he asked.

"Did you just trade my future for"—Gru could barely get the words out—"a rock with googly eyes?"

"Uh...si?" Otto smiled.

"Okay. Otto, where was this birthday party?" Gru asked.

Otto was quiet for a moment. He started babbling, but then he kind of trailed off. He just shrugged. Gru couldn't believe it—Otto didn't even know where the party had been.

"This is unacceptable," Gru said angrily. "Unacceptable! I told you guys that you weren't ready for the big leagues, and you have proven me correct!"

Gru yanked the rock from Otto's hand and darted around the lair, packing up his belongings. Otto kept babbling on, trying to make it better, but Gru couldn't stand listening to him.

"All you do is mess everything up!" Gru yelled.

"Up?" asked Josh, one of the Minion DJs, not getting it. "Pumpa Dup!"

He started playing "Get Down Tonight" by KC and The Sunshine Band on the turntable. None of the Minions danced or sang. They were panicked, convinced that Gru was leaving them forever.

"Josh!" the other Minion DJ yelled. "No playa la musica!"

The DJ smacked Josh, and Josh finally turned off the peppy song.

"You do not belong here," Gru said, glancing

around at the Minions. He'd tried to be nice about it, but they hadn't understood. Now he was going to have to be cruel to be kind. "You're fired! I'm going to find that stone. And when I get home, you all better be gone!"

The Minions gasped. Their eyes went wider than usual, and their tiny mouths trembled in fear. Was this really happening? Did Gru just fire them?

"But Mini Boss...," Otto tried.

"And Otto?" Gru yelled right in the Minion's face. "Close your yapper!"

Gru stormed upstairs, more furious than he'd ever been before. He couldn't believe he'd pulled off the perfect jewel heist only to have Otto lose the jewel. Now he'd never be able to get into the Vicious 6—and they'd be his enemies for life.

"Gru, no parta!" a small voice called out.

Gru turned and saw Kevin following him. "Por favor! Por favor!"

Gru stopped at the front door, the slightest pang of guilt overtaking him.

"Kevin, no," he finally said. "I will be better off on my own."

Gru walked out across the front lawn. At some point since he'd gotten home, it had started raining, and the water came down in sheets, drenching him. He tucked the rock into his jacket, hating that this was all he had left of his big day. A rock with silly googly eyes glued on it.

He knew Kevin was still in the window, watching him, but he didn't want to turn around. He didn't care. He'd be better off without him and Stuart and all the rest of the Minions. They were kind of good at building things, but they were terrible at the real missions a big-time villain had to go out on.

He stared down at the ground, hardly noticing the orange van that sped up the street. It slowed down, and a burly guy reached out the door and grabbed him. Before Gru could even fight back, the burly guy threw him into the back of the van, and they drove away.

CHAPTER 8

Gru couldn't see anything. Someone had shoved him into a burlap sack. He was sure it was over. The Vicious 6 had found him, and they were going to make him pay for stealing from them. He couldn't argue that he'd just wanted to show them what a great villain he was. He didn't even have the Stone anymore!

"I'm sorry," he shouted through the bag. "I

thought you'd be impressed. Could I just speak to Belle Bottom?"

Then someone picked up the burlap sack and threw him onto the floor with a *THUNK!* He peered out of the sack, trying to figure out where he was. It was a room he didn't recognize. Some sort of balcony. Then he saw the old man with the goofy dentures and wrinkly smile.

"Wild Knuckles?" he said, recognizing his hero. "You're alive?! Wow. My favorite villain is also my kidnapper? This could be a great opportunity if you don't kill me."

Wild Knuckles snapped, "Shut up and give me the Stone."

"Oh yes, the Stone," Gru said slowly. "Here's the thing about that. Kind of a funny story—"

"Give it to him!" one of the henchmen yelled.

Gru hopped over to Wild Knuckles in his sack. He went slower than he even thought possible, taking tiny baby hops.

Gru stalled, hopping just another inch forward. One of the henchmen was so annoyed he just picked up the sack and carried him the rest of the way. "And it's all going to go south very quickly," Gru continued.

He handed Wild Knuckles the rock from his pocket. Wild Knuckles turned it around and stared into the rock's little googly eyes.

"What the heck is this?" Wild Knuckles asked.

Gru couldn't answer him. Wild Knuckles nodded to his three henchmen. One grabbed Gru and threw him to another on the balcony, who dangled him over the railing. The henchman shook him by his ankles.

"Where is it, boy?" Wild Knuckles demanded.

"I don't have it! I don't have it!" Gru shouted.

"I know you're hiding it somewhere," the henchman said, shaking him again.

"I'm not! I'm not!" Gru yelled. "I swear!

Cross my heart and hope to die, stick a needle in my eye! Don't actually do that, though."

Wild Knuckles studied him.

"Somebody bring me a phone," he finally said. Seconds later, one henchman ran in with a phone. Wild Knuckles offered it to Gru. "Call home. It's ransom time."

"No, no, no," Gru said. "My mom will probably pay you to keep me."

Wild Knuckles just laughed. Then his face was serious. "Good one. Call."

He shoved the phone into Gru's hands. Gru, still hanging upside down from his ankles, dialed each number at a glacial pace, his finger circling the rotary phone. He passed it back to Wild Knuckles as it rang on the other end of the line.

"Bello!" Kevin said. "La casa de Mini Boss?"

Behind him, the Minions had set up a war room, with maps and clues of where to find

Gru. Red string zigzagged across a haphazard route, though Stuart and Bob still didn't know what the destination was.

"Who is this?" Wild Knuckles demanded.

"Kevin. Kevin le Minion."

"Kevin le what?" Wild Knuckles asked.

"Le Minion."

"You kidding me?" Wild Knuckles asked, turning back to Gru. "You got henchmen?"

Gru closed his eyes. He'd been hoping his mom would answer. At least she was a competent, responsible person. She wouldn't have been happy about this whole kidnapping business, but she might know how to get him out of it. The Minions, on the other hand, would just make everything so much worse.

"Well, that's the end of that," Gru said.

"Listen, you," Wild Knuckles growled. "Bring the Stone to me in San Francisco: 6830 Green Street. You got it? Now you got two days, or you're never going to see your little boss again!"

Wild Knuckles slammed the receiver down into its cradle. He stared at Gru, an evil smile creeping over his face. He'd given the Minions a hard deadline. He'd told them to bring him the Stone or else. They'd have to get all the way to San Francisco, and they had just two days to do it.

Gru closed his eyes, knowing the truth.

He was completely and utterly doomed.

CHAPTER 9

"Bello? Bello?" Kevin shouted into the phone. He waited a long time before hanging up. He turned to the crowd of Minions who'd formed around him.

"Buddies! La polenta! La stona!" Then he narrowed his eyes at Otto. "Otto! A donde la stona?"

Otto clenched his teeth. If only he could remember where that birthday party was or who he'd traded the Stone with. It felt as if it had happened a hundred years ago. It all seemed like a blur.

The Minions went to work. Stuart began a relentless interrogation of Otto, asking him where he was and what he was doing when he last saw the Stone. Stuart aimed a blinding light into Otto's eyes, trying to get out any secrets Otto might've been hiding.

Meanwhile, Bob pulled out his pencil and sketch pad. He drew different sketches according to what Otto said, but none of them were right. He drew Gene Simmons from KISS. Otto shook his head no. Stuart got so frustrated he jumped on top of Otto and tried to knock some sense into him. Kevin had to step in and pull him off.

"La, la, la, la," Kevin yelled, accidentally shaking Otto even harder. "Stuart, calma."

Finally, Bob used Otto's description to draw a picture of an eight-year-old boy. Bob had seen the kid around before and had a real gut instinct about this guy. Something was up with the kid. What kind of monster gives away their googly-eyed rock?

Bob flipped the drawing around and showed Otto.

"Si le! La popura!" Otto yelled. "Si le! Si le!"

Bob smiled. He'd hit the nail on the head.

It was just who he thought it was.

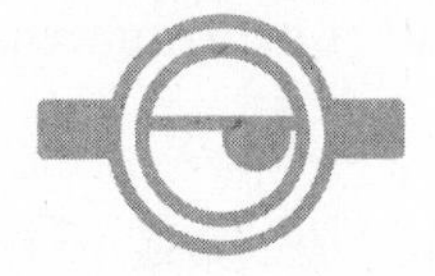

When the Minions got to the boy's house, they walked up to the front door. They could see their suspect through the living room window. He was bouncing around on a pogo stick. He had a huge pouf of hair, and it moved this way and that as he bounced.

"Otto!" Kevin whispered. "Mucho la todo muca la stona?"

"Si! Si!" Otto said. They had a positive identification.

"Okay." Kevin urged the Minions inside. "Go, go, go!"

Stuart and Bob raced forward, with Kevin following close behind. They hardly noticed that Otto stayed by the garage. They snuck in a back door and were soon face-to-face with the boy. He seemed completely unfazed by the Minions. He kept jumping around on his pogo stick.

"Oh, the rock?" he said, when Kevin asked him about it.

"Si, repeto," Kevin said. "Donde pa pira ca stona?"

"Gave that to my uncle." The kid shrugged. "It's more his style."

That was not the answer Kevin was looking for. He couldn't help himself. He started yelling, trying to get more information out of the boy, who kept jumping around on that silly pogo stick.

"I don't know where he went, you stupid Twinkies!" the boy said.

Before Stuart knew what he was doing, he kicked a skateboard that was on the floor nearby. It flew forward, and the boy bounced right on top of it. He sailed toward the ceiling fan, and a huge chunk of his hair got chopped off. Then he fell onto the table with a thud.

"Uh...okay." Kevin tiptoed toward the door. "Heh, heh. Truce."

They rushed out, trying to get away from the boy as fast as possible. Was it really Stuart's fault that he'd bounced on the skateboard? Shouldn't he have been more careful?

The Minions darted out into the street just as a bus pulled past. SAN FRANCISCO, a sign on the bus read, with a picture of the Golden Gate Bridge. Kevin suddenly knew what they had to do.

"San Panpisco," he said. "Go eh get le Gru! In San Panpisco! Vamos!"

"No. No vamos," Stuart disagreed. "Getta la stona."

"No, no, no," Kevin said. "La stona es bye-bye. Getta le Gru."

Couldn't Stuart see? There was no way they were going to find the Stone now. It was gone. They had no idea who that kid's uncle was or where they could find him. They *did* know where Gru was, though. And they still might be able to save him if they left now.

"No, stona," Stuart repeated.

"*GRUUUUUUUU!*" Kevin yelled at the top of his lungs.

"Okay, okay," Stuart finally agreed. "Jeez."

"Eh, le Otto?" Bob asked, looking around. They hadn't seen the little guy since they'd been outside the fence, watching the pogo stick kid. Where had he gone? It was as if he'd completely vanished.

"No, musta getta la Gru!" Kevin said, racing down the street. Bob and Stuart followed. "Komey! Getta la Gru!"

Bob glanced around the empty street one last time, hoping for signs of Otto. Then he sprinted after his friends.

MINIONS
MINIONS

CHAPTER 10

San Francisco was not an easy place to get to, especially if you had short, stumpy legs that could carry you only so far. So the Minions' first stop was the airport. They approached the ticket counter, and Kevin jumped up onto two suitcases to get face-to-face with the agent.

"Bello!" he said. "Tre ticketas, por San Panpisco."

"San Francisco?" the woman said, putting

down her magazine. "Okay, how will you be paying?"

Kevin bit his lip. He hadn't quite thought that far ahead. The Minions didn't have money. That was usually Gru's or Gru's mom's thing.

"No problema!" Bob yelled. He popped onto the counter and deposited a handful of loose coins and buttons.

"Oh great!" the woman said, going into full sarcasm mode. "You know, if you have any hairballs, we can upgrade you to first class!"

She grabbed her magazine and covered her face with it.

"Get out," she said coldly.

Bob picked up his loose change and buttons with a sticky lollipop. Kevin stared at the woman, wondering if she'd cave, but it seemed unlikely. Two pilots strode past in their uniforms. They had that groovy seventies style the Minions admired—big hair, big mustaches, lots of curly tufts sticking out from the top of their collars.

Across the way, another group of pilots and flight attendants chatted. They'd left a whole pile of luggage unattended—luggage that presumably held some pilot and flight-attendant uniforms. Kevin glanced sideways at the other Minions. Did they see what he saw? This was their chance.

They crept up beside the group and yanked some of the bags away. It would be a while before anyone realized they were gone.

Freshly uniformed, Captain Kevin and First Mate Stuart sat in the cockpit. They checked and rechecked the buttons in front of them, even though they had no clue what any of them did. Stuart yanked on a big red lever just for fun.

"Okay," Kevin said. "Vamos."

Kevin studied the manual, trying to figure out the first thing they had to do. Stuart spun around in his chair and grabbed the radio. "Bello," he said into the intercom. "Soy Stuart Smith, le captain, qui le komay."

In the cabin behind them, Bob strode down the aisle handing out single peanuts. He was dressed as a female flight attendant. They'd found only two pilot uniforms and one flight-attendant uniform in the suitcases, and Bob looked the best in heels.

Kevin thumbed through the manual. He was determined to find step one of piloting, but Stuart was impatient. He jabbed at the controls some more, even though Kevin specifically told him not to. The oxygen masks fell from the ceiling. Then the wheels went up and down, up and down. Finally, Stuart pressed a giant red button, and the engines whirred to life.

The plane shot forward and raced toward the control tower, nearly smashing right into it. But Kevin pulled back on the yoke, and the plane took flight. They just barely missed the tower.

They'd done it—they were flying! As soon as they were in the air, Stuart's face turned green. He ran to the bathroom to puke, leaving Kevin to pilot the aircraft alone. He didn't really have to do much now that they were cruising, so he just put on his eye mask and went to sleep.

When he woke up an hour later, alarms were going off all around him. Stuart still hadn't come back from the bathroom. San Francisco had appeared on the digital map in front of him, and now he had to descend. He'd have to land this thing.

He just jammed the controls forward. It turned out that was not the right move, because the plane nose-dived toward the ground. Kevin lifted out of his seat as if he were on a roller coaster. He could hear the passengers screaming behind him. He pulled at the controls hard, and the plane did a giant loop the loop in the sky. He jammed the controls forward again, and the plane began to nose-dive once more.

He saw the ground in front of him. They were headed straight toward it.

At the very last second, he yanked the controls again, and the plane righted itself. He managed a smooth landing across the runway. All the passengers cheered.

"*Woohoooo!*" Kevin yelled. "Haha!"

After Kevin stopped cheering, Stuart appeared in the doorway behind him. He was covered in toilet paper, and he had that gross blue liquid from planes' toilets inside his goggle.

"No," he snapped, glaring at Kevin. "No, haha."

CHAPTER 11

The Minions trudged up a steep San Francisco hill. Kevin studied the map, realizing they still had miles and miles to go. These hills were no joke. With every step, the Minions were more certain they'd pass out from exhaustion before they ever found Gru.

Just then, Bob tripped and rolled down the hill. With a few bumps and skips, he was gone, disappearing far below. Kevin and Stuart ran after him, but a trolley was now barreling up the giant hill. They froze right in the middle of the tracks, terrified they were about to get run over.

"Bello! Komey!" yelled a familiar voice.

Bob was riding the trolley up the hill. His backpack had gotten hooked on it, and now he was perched in the front seat, right next to the conductor. Bob rang the trolley's bell. Kevin and Stuart darted under the trolley car and grabbed the back of it. They were barely holding on. Stuart clung to Kevin's overalls, pulling them down so his butt was showing.

"Next stop, Green Street!" the conductor called out.

When the trolley finally stopped, Bob hopped off. Kevin and Stuart darted out from underneath. They were at the address that Wild Knuckles had mentioned on the phone. A giant WK marked the villain's lair.

The Minions scurried around the side of the

house and peered over the brick wall. They could see Gru inside the house through a window. Three burly guys sparred on the grass. Just one look at them, and Stuart jumped down from his perch, wanting to give up. The henchmen were huge. The Minions didn't stand a chance.

Kevin started arguing with him. Why had they come so far just to leave now? They were so close.... They had to save Gru! As the two went back and forth, Bob found an old can of orange spray paint and accidentally sprayed himself in the face. That gave Kevin an idea. Maybe they could sneak past the henchmen in disguise....

Kevin yanked a bush from the ground and wore that. Bob climbed inside a flowerpot so he could hide. Stuart painted himself orange so he blended in with the brick wall, but he was not happy about it. Why was his disguise the only one that involved head-to-toe body paint?

They tiptoed past the henchmen outside. Just when they thought they'd completely fooled them, Bob sneezed.

"Hey...wait a minute...," one of the henchmen said. He grabbed the flowerpot, revealing Bob inside it. Kevin and Stuart ran to help Bob, but then they were in real trouble.

"Trespassers! Get them!" the henchman yelled.

The Minions fled the yard, with the henchmen close behind. The henchmen gave chase down a narrow street and cornered them outside a place called Master Chow Acupuncture.

"Gotcha now," one of the henchmen said.

"Time to break some bones," another said.

The three henchmen attacked, using different styles of martial arts. Kevin tried his best to fight his henchman, but he was getting creamed. Every time he was about to land a punch, he got socked in the gut or kicked in the face or punted like a football. He crashed into a store window and saw an older woman inside, performing acupuncture on one of her clients. Kevin stared at her, his eyes wide.

"Help-a!" he wailed.

In less than a minute, the woman was outside. She glared at the three hulking henchmen. "You like picking on little guys, huh?" she asked.

"Ha!" The henchmen laughed. "Go take a nap, old lady."

Master Chow was about to go inside, but she slowed her steps. Then she turned back and narrowed her eyes at the henchmen. "Old lady?" she asked.

In a split second, the woman kicked a wooden stool out from beside the door. It hit one of the henchmen in the chest, and he caught it. Then she did a quick series of jumps and kicks, sending the henchman flying backward and putting a hole right in the brick wall in front of Wild Knuckles's lair. For a brief moment, flames rose up around her.

"You should address me with respect," she said. "I am a master of the ancient Shaolin art of kung fu."

Before they could respond, Master Chow executed a complicated series of jumps, punches, and kicks, knocking the other two henchmen to the ground. Then she turned and walked away without even breaking a sweat.

"Whoa, Bella," Stuart said.

"Get lost!" she called over her shoulder at the henchmen.

Then Master Chow disappeared back into her office, leaving the Minions alone with the men. The three burly guys were too beaten and bruised to fight anymore. They slunk off down the street, turning back one last time.

"If you come back to our place, you're dead!" one yelled to Kevin.

When the henchmen were finally gone, Kevin gazed longingly at where Master Chow had disappeared. This woman, this master of kung fu, was exactly what they needed. They'd never seen someone vanquish another human being so quickly. Maybe she could teach them to be fierce fighting machines . . . or at least competent enough so Gru would take them back.

"Komey! Le mooka no sa comprehenda kung fu!" Kevin said.

Stuart and Bob followed him inside, and the door slammed shut behind them.

"Oh pank you!" Kevin raved as he walked right into Master Chow's treatment room. He ignored the client who was half naked on Master Chow's acupuncture table.

"Shh, shh. You can thank me by going away," Master Chow whispered. "I'm working."

Kevin started rambling about kung fu, and how they needed to get Gru, and how she would be the perfect teacher for them. He made some fighting gestures with his hands.

"*You* want to learn kung fu?" Master Chow asked, looking the tiny Minion up and down. She laughed as if that were the funniest thing she'd ever heard.

Stuart pushed Kevin aside and stepped forward, thinking he could convince Master Chow himself. He gave her his most sultry stare.

"Bello, chica," Stuart said softly. "Teacha nu kung fu? Pour smoochy, smoochy?"

Master Chow pressed a needle into the client's back, and he smacked Stuart in the face. Stuart hit the client back. Then Master Chow inserted another needle, and the client punched

Stuart five different ways, eventually knocking him across the room. Bob watched the whole thing, convinced that maybe Stuart just didn't know how to talk to Master Chow. Maybe Bob would be the one to persuade her to help them.

"My teaching days are over," Master Chow said. "This is my life now."

Bob's eyes filled with tears. He stepped forward, and Stuart and Kevin joined him, trying to make themselves cry, too. They needed to save their Mini Boss. How could they possibly do it without her?

"Fine." Master Chow finally sighed. "I will teach you."

The Minions jumped up and down, thrilled by the news.

MINIONS
MINIONS

CHAPTER 12

Back at Gru's house, Dave the Minion was dressed as a seventies housewife with a huge beehive hairdo. He walked around serving deviled eggs. Gru's mom was throwing a Tupperware party, even though the Minions didn't know what Tupperware was.

The living room was packed with friends of Gru's mom. The women wore stylish flowered shift dresses and knee-high boots, and some were in flare jeans and crop tops. Their hair was so teased that it was twice as big as usual.

"The name of the game is SELL SELL SELL!" Gru's mom shouted. Then she shooed the Minions into the living room. She didn't seem to notice that Gru had disappeared. He hadn't been around much lately regardless. He was always in his room or downstairs in the lair, which she knew nothing about.

Mel, another one of the Minions, did a demonstration in front of the entire group. Three Minions stood beside him. They were all dressed in seventies outfits and wore huge, teased wigs. Mel pressed the lid of the plastic food container, and the lid made a burping noise. The ladies laughed. The other three Minions joined in, and soon they were a Tupperware burp chorus, making all sorts of burping noises. They were having so much fun it took them a second to realize a giant hole had just been torn in the roof.

The Vicious 6's Super Ship hovered in the sky above. One by one they rappelled down into Gru's living room. The housewives collected their Tupperware and ran out the door as fast as possible, leaving Gru's mom and the Minions behind.

"Where's Gru?" Belle Bottom yelled as she dropped into the living room.

"Huh? How should I know?" Gru's mom asked. She studied the rest of the Vicious 6. "What's with the costumes? Halloween was four months ago. You look stupid. Buzz off! Shoo!"

Gru's mom started throwing Tupperware containers at the Vicious 6, trying to get them out of her house.

"I'm getting my meat tenderizer!" she yelled.

Nun-Chuck stalked forward. "Let me help you with that, dearie."

"Nuh-uh! Don't touch me!" Gru's mom said, darting away from her.

Nun-Chuck chased Gru's mom into the kitchen just as Belle Bottom spotted the Minions.

"Now... where's the boy?" Belle Bottom asked. She dropped down to look them in their googly little eyes. Mel was so terrified he started shaking.

"Oh, I didn't mean to scare you," Belle Bottom said. "Don't worry. We're not mad at him. We just want to... hire him."

"Oh," Mel said, hemming and hawing. "Ah, well... la Mini Boss partito..."

Apparently, that wasn't a good answer. Jean-Clawed grabbed Mel and shook him.

"WHERE IS HE?" he yelled into Mel's face.

"Wild Knuckles!" Mel screeched. "San Panpisco!"

"Wild Knuckles is alive?" Jean-Clawed asked, tossing Mel aside. They'd left him in that jungle in the middle of nowhere, with no way out, hoping they'd never see him again. How did he survive? He was a million years old!

"And working with the kid," Belle Bottom said. "*Hmmmm.* We're going to San Francisco. Let's hit it!"

She straightened up and looked around at her team. If Wild Knuckles was alive, they knew exactly where to find him...and Gru. It wouldn't be long now before the Stone was hers again.

The rope dropped down from the Super Ship, and Belle Bottom and her team grabbed on, zooming back up into the sky. Gru's mom hopped in from the kitchen. Nun-Chuck had tied her hands and legs so she couldn't get away. She stared at the aircraft above as the Vicious 6 disappeared on it.

"You had better be paying for my roof!" she yelled after them.

MINIONS
MINIONS

CHAPTER 13

Otto pedaled as fast as his little legs could. The road ahead was long. The sun beat down on him, soaking his clothes with sweat. He was so thirsty his throat was on fire.

"*Stona . . . stona . . .* ," he chanted to himself.

Vultures circled overhead. Rattlesnakes slithered along the road, hissing at him. He tried to keep up his pace, but he was so tired. He'd been traveling on the toy trike forever.

He didn't know how long he could keep going through this horrible desert. There was nothing in any direction.

He missed his friends, but he knew he was on one of the most important missions a Minion could have. While Kevin, Stuart, and Bob had gone inside to find the birthday party kid, he'd seen the boy's uncle zoom out of the garage on a motorcycle. The uncle was wearing the Zodiac Stone around his neck. Otto had grabbed a toy tricycle, and he'd been following the biker ever since, though he'd lost sight of him a while back.

He kept going, pedaling slower and slower. His legs were tired. He felt dizzy. Otto looked up at the sun and was amazed to find that it had turned into the Zodiac Stone. It was there, ready for him to take it. Otto reached up, up, up, and felt his fingers wrap around the Stone. . . .

Then he was shaking. A pair of arms smacked him and shook him until his eyes jolted open and he was staring up at a huge, muscular man. The biker he'd followed into the desert—was it really him? Or was Otto hallucinating again?

"Dude!" the biker said, smiling a big, glittery smile. He had braces just like Otto did. "I thought we lost you there for a minute."

Otto groaned. He looked at his hand, fingers still curled around some object hanging from the biker's neck. Otto was shocked. The Stone! It was right there! Otto started pawing at it, trying to tug it off.

"Okay, okay. You wanna try this on?" The biker laughed. He pulled it off his neck and put it around Otto's.

"Yeah, yeah, yeah!" Otto said cheerfully. "La stonaaaaaaa!"

The biker held him away from the hot pavement. Even though the man looked kind of scary, he was sweet. He grinned at Otto with his braces-smile.

"Hey, hey, hey, soul brother. Where you jettin' off to?" the biker asked.

"Uh, le palimo a San Panpisco!" Otto said as the biker helped him to his feet.

"San Francisco? Frisco Disco!" the biker said. "It's your lucky day, kid. I'm headed up the coast. I could drop you off along the way."

Otto nodded. The biker set him down on the back of his motorcycle, leaving the plastic toy trike behind. With a loud *ROAR!* of the engine, they were off.

"Yeehaw!" Otto yelled at the top of his lungs.

CHAPTER 14

"We begin with a basic kick." Master Chow stood on a mat in the center of her training room. Her leg shot out into the air. "Hi-yah! Now you."

The Minions tried to kick the same way Master Chow had, but their legs were too short. They could barely get their kicks to her knee height. Bob tried so hard he fell over.

"Okay, no kicking," Master Chow said. She

went over to a weapon display and pulled out what looked like a giant maraca. "This is a melon hammer. It's a weapon."

She approached a wooden dummy. "This is Fred. He is a dummy," she said, then smiled at him as if they were old pals. "Never underestimate a dummy."

Stuart scoffed. "Dummy."

Bob stared at the faceless mound. He waved to him. "Bello, Fred!"

"Now attack!" Master Chow yelled.

Stuart launched forward, knocking Kevin over in the process. He went all out on the mannequin, hitting and kicking him, but the dummy kept spinning around on his base, hitting Stuart back. *WHAP!* In one quick blow, he smacked Stuart's goggle deep into his head. The Minion had to let out a breath to get it out.

Bob cheered Stuart on, but Master Chow

was not impressed. She walked over to a stack of wooden boards.

"Doubt tells me I cannot break this wood," she said. "But doubt exists only in the mind. You know what I say to my mind?"

She stared down at the boards, concentrating on them, and then smashed the boards with her head, breaking them in two.

"Now you," she said, gesturing to the Minions.

Kevin hit the boards with his head, but he just fell over. Stuart tried to use Kevin's head instead of his own, which really ticked Kevin off. He was tired of Stuart always goofing on him. He turned to walk away when—*PING!*—an acupuncture needle landed in his neck. He froze. He couldn't move an inch.

"Okay," Master Chow said, pleased with herself. "Clearly, we are not ready for philosophy. Let's just train."

The Minions lined up in a row to continue

practicing their punches and kicks. First, Kevin started making kung fu noises, and then Bob joined in time to the beat. They kept going, making music together, and Stuart grabbed a boom box and started in, too. Stuart danced to the beat, until Master Chow staff smacked him with her staff.

Stuart stopped for a second... but only until Master Chow left. Then the Minions went back to their dance. Master Chow ran in and smacked Kevin and Stuart when she realized they were at it again.

"Ow! Blumach!" Kevin yelled.

Bob flinched, but Master Chow just patted him on the head.

"Rest up," she said. "Tomorrow's going to be even worse."

These Minions' names are Kevin, Bob, and Stuart. Together, they make a great team.

This is Otto. He's new to the Minion crew. His stories are *very* long.

There are so many other Minions! They all have one goal: to work for a despicable master.

Luckily, the Minions work for Gru. He wants to become a great supervillain. He is such a good Mini Boss!

One day, Gru has an interview with the Vicious 6. They're the evilest supervillain team in the world! But first Gru must find their secret lair hidden inside a record store.

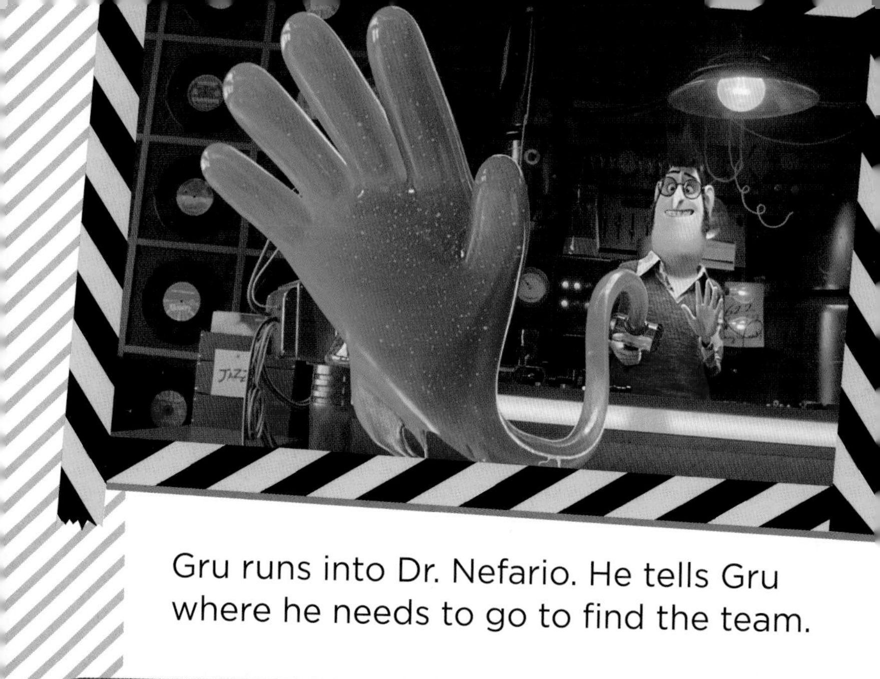

Gru runs into Dr. Nefario. He tells Gru where he needs to go to find the team.

Dr. Nefario also gives Gru his very first gadget. It's a green hand that sticks to everything!

Gru is so excited to meet the Vicious 6! He has been dreaming of this moment for years.

They are Stronghold, Svengeance, Nun-Chuck, Jean-Clawed, and Belle Bottom. Wild Knuckles used to be their leader.

But when Gru suddenly disappears, the Minions must rescue him. Will the Minions be able to pilot a plane and learn kung fu to save their Mini Boss?

The next day, the Minions stood in the center of a redwood forest. Master Chow was nowhere to be seen.

"Many fighters have asked me, how did I become a great master?" she said from somewhere above them. They looked up and finally spotted her in one of the massive trees. She was standing on a branch. She sprinted across it and jumped, twisting like an Olympic diver. She landed right in front of them.

"I realized even the smallest of us are capable of great things if we can find our inner beast. You just dig down deep. Feel the strength within your heart. And..." She yelled so loud it shook the trees. Flames briefly surrounded her again. Leaves fell down around them.

"Uh, gesundheit," Stuart said.

"Now you try," she said.

Kevin tried, but when he yelled, it came out more like a cough. Stuart's attempt sounded as if he were blowing a raspberry. Bob made the cutest little roar.

Master Chow just sighed. She seemed a little disappointed in the Minions. Then she sprinted off into the forest, running so fast her feet lit up the dried leaves beneath them. She turned and flew through the air toward Stuart, her leg stretched out in front of her.

"Find your inner beast!" she called to him. "Stop this kick!"

Bob and Kevin rushed out of the way, but Stuart wasn't sure what to do. What did she mean, *find your inner beast*? He stared at Master Chow's foot, which was flying at his face.

BLAMMMM!

Master Chow kicked him hard, sending him flying through the redwood trees.

He definitely had not found his inner beast.

CHAPTER 15

While the Minions were perfecting their kung fu, Wild Knuckles had tied Gru to a contraption he called the Disco Inferno. The giant spinning record was a torture device. With each rotation of the record, Gru came closer and closer to a spinning blade. It would be only a few more hours before the blade tore him apart.

"*How do you like it, how do you like it . . . ,*" the song on the record played.

Gru was dizzy. He wasn't sure how long

he'd been tied to this stupid thing. It had been hours, maybe days. The song kept playing on repeat, and his head hurt. Finally, it stopped.

"Is this heaven?" he asked, bleary-eyed.

Wild Knuckles stood over him. Apparently, he'd turned off the Disco Inferno. "I just had to fire my henchmen," he said. "You know why? 'Cause they weren't getting the job done."

Gru couldn't help noticing that Wild Knuckles didn't seem very happy about firing his henchmen. In fact, he seemed kind of...sad.

"Okay," Wild Knuckles continued. "I'm just gonna untie you now because I—uh—I need you to do some stuff for me around the house. And it might be, ya know, kind of nice to have a little company around here."

Wild Knuckles pulled him off the giant record, but Gru was still so dizzy he couldn't walk. He stumbled to the floor.

"Oh. Oh yeah," he said, the room spinning

around him. "Two villains just doing some chores. Who knows what kind of trouble we could get into?"

Gru got to his feet and laughed as he fell again.

"What's that? That's your evil chuckle?" Wild Knuckles asked.

"Obviously."

"Well, it stinks!" he said. "You sound like a clown who swallowed a kazoo."

Gru stood up straight. He couldn't let Wild Knuckles talk to him that way.

"Well, you look like a wizard going through an end-of-life crisis."

"Easy there, Don Rickles," Wild Knuckles said as he kicked Gru through the door.

"Who's Don Rickles?" Gru asked.

An hour later, Gru was standing over Wild Knuckles's pool with a net and a bucket. Wild Knuckles had spread out on a lounge chair. Every inch of his wrinkly, old body was covered with tanning oil, and he held a foil tanning reflector in his hands. Gru could see the alley through a hole in the brick wall surrounding the yard, but he didn't dare make a break for it. Not with Wild Knuckles watching him.

"Start with the pool. This place has gotta be spick-and-span," the elderly villain said.

"What are you doing?" Gru asked. "You look like the overcooked turkey my mom makes on Thanksgiving."

Gru stood over the pool, chuckling at his own joke. Suddenly, a crocodile snapped at the bucket, breaking it in two.

"Oh yeah," Wild Knuckles said. "I forgot

to mention—the pool is filled with my pet crocodiles!"

"Yeah, well... doesn't scare me." Gru tried to put on a brave face. "You should meet my dog."

Another crocodile reared its head and almost decapitated Gru.

"Be careful!" Wild Knuckles yelled across the yard. "I can't have you lose an arm, because I need you to change some light bulbs after this. Here, let me show you how it's done."

Wild Knuckles went to the pool and grabbed the net out of Gru's hands. He dipped it into the water, and another crocodile jumped up, snapping at him.

"Betsy, knock it off!" he said. "We've been in a fight since I stopped feeding them live bait."

Wild Knuckles tried to skim the top of the

pool, but one of the other crocodiles bit down on the net. It yanked the net hard to the side. Wild Knuckles stumbled, then lost his balance. In one swift motion, he fell directly into the pool.

"Marvin! No! No! Stop that!" he yelled as the crocodiles circled him. One snapped viciously, just missing his arm. Another went for his head. Wild Knuckles flailed in the water. He looked like he was drowning.

Gru glanced back at the hole in the brick wall. The alley—and his freedom—were right on the other side. He knew this was his chance to get away. But Wild Knuckles would never make it out of the pool if he left now....

"Help! Oh, oh!" Wild Knuckles cried.

Gru glanced at Wild Knuckles and then at the exit. He didn't want to be stuck in this place forever. But how could he leave like this?

"The net!" he yelled, pointing to the pool

net still in Wild Knuckles's hand. Wild Knuckles handed it to him, and Gru was sure he'd be able to reel him in. Then a crocodile came over and chomped down on it, breaking the net.

Now Wild Knuckles was sinking. They had no way to save him. Gru ran to the diving board. In one quick jump, he landed on a crocodile's head. He reached out to Wild Knuckles. "Take my hand!" he yelled.

Gru yanked as hard as he could. The crocodile reared its head, and in an instant, Wild Knuckles and Gru went flying. Then they landed in a dripping, wet heap on the grass.

"You could've run," Wild Knuckles said when he finally caught his breath. "But you—you didn't."

"I told you," Gru said softly. "You are my favorite villain in the world. I could not let you get eaten by crocodiles, even though that would have been kind of cool to watch."

"So you want to be a great villain, huh?" Wild Knuckles asked.

"That's all I ever wanted," Gru said.

Wild Knuckles looked down, deep in thought. "You want, uh, I don't know. You want me—you want me to teach you a thing or two?"

Gru smiled so big his face hurt. Yes—the answer was yes.

CHAPTER 16

Wild Knuckles put on a pair of glasses. Then he looked out the van window, surveilling their surroundings.

"First rule of heists: Always stay in character," he said. He was wearing a sweatshirt that said WORLD'S GREATEST GRANDPA. "You got that, *grandson*?"

"Got it, Grandpa," Gru said, trying to pretend. He was wearing a Boy Scout uniform Wild Knuckles had found for him.

The pair strode into the bank. Gru followed close behind Wild Knuckles, paying attention to every little thing the villain did. He couldn't believe he had a chance to learn from his hero. He was actually robbing a bank with *Wild Knuckles*.

"Say, do you mind if we use the john?" Wild Knuckles asked when he found a bank clerk. "Poindexter here can't hold it until we get home."

The clerk showed them to the bathroom, and Wild Knuckles walked right up to one of the urinals. An eye scanner came out of the wall and scanned his iris. In an instant, the walls slid back, revealing another room. BANK OF EVIL read a sign on the wall.

"The Bank of Evil," Gru breathed.

"It's showtime, kid. Follow my lead, and don't forget your cue," Wild Knuckles said as they strode up to a bank teller with huge shoulders and a round, bulbous nose. Wild Knuckles slid a check across the counter. "I just need to cash this."

"Wowee zowee," Gru said, getting into character. "What a big bank! How many security guards are in here?"

Wild Knuckles glared at Gru. "Well, that's my grandson"—he tried to smile—"who still hasn't learned that children should be seen and not heard."

The bank teller showed the pair a framed photo on his desk and proceeded to tell Gru and Wild Knuckles about his baby son, Vector, who was *not* cute. In the middle of their exchange, Wild Knuckles suddenly grabbed his chest. His eyes went wide.

"Help!" he yelled as he stumbled to the ground. "I'm seeing a white light! Helen, I'm coming for ya!"

Gru stood there, dumbstruck. Wild Knuckles

stared at him, waiting for him to say something, but Gru was so stunned by the scene unfolding in front of him he'd forgotten his line. What was he supposed to say, again?

"Helen, I'm coming for ya!" Wild Knuckles repeated. This time he looked directly at Gru, like *THIS IS THE CUE I WAS TALKING ABOUT.*

"Oh." Gru finally remembered. "Help! Help my—my pop pop!"

The bank teller ran out from behind his desk. Gru darted to the stairs and tugged at the guards standing at the bottom of them, hoping he could lure them away. A crowd surrounded Wild Knuckles as he twitched on the floor. Once the guards went to check on Wild Knuckles, Gru was able to go up the stairs toward the vault.

"Help!" Wild Knuckles yelled. "This is the

big one. Ya hear that? It's the sweet sound of angels!"

Gru stood on the balcony, looking at the scene below. He pulled out the Sticky Hand the man at Criminal Records had given him and aimed it at the key ring hanging from the bank teller's belt. He launched it, and the hand grabbed the ring. Still, the ring didn't budge. Wild Knuckles had to distract the teller for a few minutes so Gru could tug the keys free.

"Do something! My life is flashing before my eyes!" Wild Knuckles yelled as he grabbed the teller by the top of his shirt.

Gru finally launched the keys up to the balcony and used them to open the vault. It took a few tries before he could move the heavy vault door. At first, he spun the lever in the wrong direction, and then Wild Knuckles had to yell what to do.

"The other way! The other way!" he called out. The crowd stared as Wild Knuckles flailed around to distract them.

The EMTs rushed in and started shocking him with two metal paddles.

"Don't give up on me now, buddy!" one of the EMTs yelled. She pressed the paddles to Wild Knuckles's chest, and a jolt of electricity shot through him. Wild Knuckles felt as if he were on fire. For a few seconds, he actually did see a bright white light.

"No, no, no!" Wild Knuckles tried, when they finally stopped shocking him. "I'm feeling better!"

But the EMTs shocked him one more time before Gru rushed in and stopped them. "Thank you! You saved my grandpa!" he cried as he helped Wild Knuckles to his feet.

"Did we do the heist?" Wild Knuckles asked, his eyes half closed.

Gru tried to laugh it off. "Grandpas say the darndest things." Then he tossed the keys back to the teller as they strode out of the bank. "You dropped these."

Gru didn't say anything until they were safe inside the van. He pulled an antique oil painting out of his jacket. "Look what I got!" he said.

"Not bad! Not bad at all," Wild Knuckles said, surveying their loot. "We make a good team."

"We do?" Gru asked.

"Oh yeah!" Wild Knuckles smiled. "We gotta keep at it. Wait until you see what I'm going to teach you next time."

"I cannot wait," Gru said, and he really meant it. From now on, he and Wild Knuckles would be a team. Nothing could stop them.

Wild Knuckles hit the gas, and they sped down the street. "*Yahoooo!* This is gonna be fun!"

MINIONS
MINIONS

CHAPTER 17

The Minions spent hours in the training room. They practiced elbow strikes and punched until their tiny fists hurt and their even tinier knuckles were swollen and red. Stuart attacked Fred, the training dummy, but the dummy pummeled him to the ground.

Then it was time to take their lessons outside. Master Chow taught them how to do parkour over every building and roof in San Francisco. They flipped and kicked off things and launched themselves into the air. Afterward, they went to Fisherman's Wharf and stood on wooden poles in the water, working on their balance.

The training with Master Chow went by in a blur. It felt as if they'd done hundreds of push-ups. They went back to the redwood forest. Kevin balanced on rocks while Stuart puffed a bellows at the coals under him and Bob cooked some food. They went back to the training room and practiced breaking wooden boards. With a sneeze, Bob was finally able to break a board with his head. Master Chow was so happy to see this that she dropped more heavy things on his head to see how he'd react. After convincing Kevin and Bob to play along, Stuart showed Master Chow his "wind punch" and how he could knock Kevin and Bob down without touching them. After so much practice, Master Chow finally made her announcement.

"Kevin, Stuart, and Bob," she said. "You are ready."

"Go-a!" Kevin yelled as he ran for the door. "Getta la Mini Boss!"

"No, no, no, no, no!" Master Chow corrected. She grabbed three blue ribbons off a nearby table. "Ready for your junior kung fu achievement badges!"

But when she turned to hand the Minions their ribbons, they were gone.

Stuart, Bob, and Kevin darted through the hole in the perimeter wall of Wild Knuckles's lair and into the dark courtyard. They struck their first kung fu pose on the lawn, half expecting the henchmen to still be there. But the yard was quiet.

The Minions snuck over to the back door.

Bob stood on top of Kevin to reach the door-knob, while Stuart stood in a fighting stance, ready to attack. Kevin and Bob threw the door open, and Stuart launched himself inside, wildly punching the air. But there was no one there.

Kevin and Bob followed Stuart through the doorway, but there was no sign of Gru. He wasn't tied up on some chair or screaming for them to help him. He wasn't anywhere.

"*Ooooooo*," Bob cooed. "Mini Boss!"

The Minions decided to split up to search for Gru, but before they got even a few steps, they heard a rumble come from outside. They looked around, trying to see what it was, when suddenly—*CRASH!*—a red, lobsterlike tank smashed through the living-room wall. It was coming straight for Kevin, its giant pincers clicking, ready to grab their next target. Kevin had to dive out the window to avoid being squashed.

Bob and Stuart ran in the opposite direction. Four other vehicles rolled in behind the tank.

The Vicious 6 climbed out of their vehicles and started searching the lair. Belle Bottom went into one room, and Svengeance went into another. Jean-Clawed, Stronghold, and Nun-Chuck ran through every inch of the house.

"They're not here!" Jean-Clawed finally yelled.

"Fan out and find them," Belle Bottom ordered.

The Vicious 6 left the lair and descended on the city. San Francisco wasn't a huge place, and they knew Wild Knuckles and Gru were here somewhere. They'd find the Zodiac Stone and take back what was theirs. How could they let some saggy, old villain stop them?

They were so focused on the mission they didn't notice Stuart, Kevin, and Bob trailing behind them.

MINIONS
MINIONS

CHAPTER 18

Wild Knuckles got to the front door first. He was still talking to Gru as he unlocked the door. "My friend," he said, "you're now going to learn from your new school."

They pushed inside and saw all the destruction. The sofa was overturned. Bricks and huge chunks of concrete were scattered over the floor. It looked as if a tornado had swept through and ripped apart everything in its path.

"Oh no..." Wild Knuckles took another step and heard a crunch. He looked down and saw a newspaper clipping, with a headline proclaiming how Wild Knuckles had founded the Vicious 6. "I can't believe they did this to me!" he yelled.

He went around the room, kicking and throwing things as if he were a little kid.

"I—I taught them everything I know!" he cried. "WE WERE A TEAM!"

Wild Knuckles sank into a chair. He looked as if he might cry. Gru hated seeing him so upset. This was one of the most powerful villains in the world! One of the most underhanded, treacherous thieves! He couldn't let this get him down.

"Hey," Gru tried. "You are a great bad guy. And they are stupid idiots."

"Only dream I ever had was doing bad stuff

with my buddies," Wild Knuckles said. "Now look at me. Old. Alone..."

"Well, you are old," Gru went on. "But you're not alone."

Wild Knuckles just grumbled.

"All right," Gru said, trying to give his most rousing pep talk. "Listen up, buster. We are starting a new team. And it's going to be called the Terrible Twos. We can find a better name later. But right now, we're going to find that stone and show everybody that you've still got it!"

But Wild Knuckles didn't even smile. He barely looked up.

"Come on," he finally said. "You're just a little kid. It's over. Go home."

"But you said we—"

"*Go home*," Wild Knuckles repeated.

Gru was stunned. All his dreams of traveling the world with Wild Knuckles, being an unstoppable crime duo—just like that, they were all gone. If Wild Knuckles couldn't be one of the Vicious 6, he wasn't going to pair up with some sixth grader. Maybe Belle Bottom was right about Gru—maybe a kid *couldn't* be a villain.

Gru slowly walked to the door, hoping Wild Knuckles would change his mind. But when he turned back, the old villain was still sitting in that chair, staring off into space. It was as if Gru weren't even there.

He walked down the front steps and out into the street. The sky was dark. For the first time in his life, he felt truly alone—he was far away from home with nowhere to go. He hadn't spoken to his mother in days. He'd fired all the Minions, and now Wild Knuckles had fired him (well, kind of). His eyes welled up with tears as he climbed onto a passing trolley.

A few streets over, a parade was making its

way through Chinatown. The trolley passed behind the parade route, and Gru noticed something small and yellow clinging to the back of a dragon puppet. He had to squint to make sure he wasn't imagining things.

"Otto?"

He jumped down from the trolley and started following the puppet, trying to get Otto's attention. "Otto! Otto! Otto!" he yelled. "It's Mini Boss!"

Otto turned and spotted Gru in the crowd. "Mini Boss!" he cried.

Otto dropped down from the dragon puppet and ran toward him. Gru climbed over the crowd, then scaled the barrier, stepping out into the parade route. Otto ran right into his arms.

"Otto!" Gru yelled again. He never thought he'd be so happy to see the little guy. Otto was technically the one who'd lost the Zodiac Stone—the one who had gotten Gru into this whole mess in the first place. None of that mattered anymore, though—not really. Gru was just so relieved to see a familiar face.

"Looka! Looka!" Otto said, holding something up in front of Gru's nose. "Cinda la stona!"

"You found the Stone?" Gru almost couldn't believe it. He stared at the jewel, which glittered in the light of the parade. "Otto, I'm so proud of you."

Otto's cheeks turned a rosy pink. He looked genuinely pleased with himself.

"All right, we don't have much time!" Gru said. "We got to get this to Wild Knuckles!"

They pushed out into the crowd, trying to get off the parade route. All Gru could think about was cheering up his old friend. How could Wild Knuckles be sad once he saw that they had the Zodiac Stone, the treasure he himself had found? How could he say he was out of the game, a washed-up has-been? Stealing the Stone had been one of his greatest accomplishments!

Gru and Otto darted down the street. They'd find Wild Knuckles, and they'd stop the Vicious 6 from whatever evil they were plotting. Working together, there'd be nothing they couldn't do.